淘气的乒乓猫

乒乒猫玩音乐

〔荷〕米斯·博豪宇斯 著   〔荷〕菲珀·维斯顿多普 绘   蒋佳惠 译

人民文学出版社
PEOPLE'S LITERATURE PUBLISHING HOUSE

女主人待会儿要上钢琴课。

她得先练习一会儿。

The Lady is going to have a piano lesson.

She needs to do some practice.

乒乓欣赏着美妙的音乐。"很好听吧，乒乓？"
"嗯，"乒乓说，"我听得都打哈欠了。"

Pom is enjoying the beautiful music. 'That's lovely eh, Pim?'
'Mmm,' says Pim. 'It's making me yawn a bit.'

哎呀！女主人弹错了。
难听极了！

Oh dear. The Lady plays the wrong note.
That sounds horrible!

"我永远也不可能学得会！"
她一边喊，一边离开房间。

'I'll never learn it!'
she cries and leaves the room.

"你觉得我也能学会吗，乒乒？"

'Do you think I could do it too, Pim?'

乒乓先把爪子放到一个琴键上，然后是下一个琴键，再下一个琴键……
"我学会了！我会弹钢琴了！"他兴高采烈地喊道。

First Pom puts his paw on one key, then the next and the next...
'Oh, I can do it! I can play the piano!' he cries out happily.

可是，乒乓一点儿也不觉得那算得上演奏。
"那怎么能算是弹钢琴呢？你只不过是在琴键上走路而已！"

But Pim doesn't think it is clever.
'That's not playing! You just walked along the keys!'

"听好了，乒乓，
我这就弹一首真正的乐曲。"

'Watch this, Pim,
I'm going to play a proper song.'

"停下，乒乒！这算什么调调呀！"
乒乒喊道。

'Pom stop! What a row!'
shouts Pim.

"这曲子好听极了，
你根本就不懂什么叫弹钢琴。"

**'It's beautiful.
You don't know the first thing about playing the piano.'**

"我要是坚持这样弹下去,
总有一天会出名的。"

'If I carry on like this,
I'll be famous.'

乒乒有一个计划，
他也要演奏音乐。

**Pim has a plan,
he is going to make music as well.**

"我在打鼓。打鼓比钢琴有趣多了。
我以后要成为一名鼓手。"

'I'm drumming. It's much more fun than piano.
I'm going to be a drummer.'

"成为一名特别出名的鼓手！"
他用力地敲打着锅子。

'And a very famous one indeed!'
and he hits the pan hard.

兵兵更加用力地弹钢琴：

"是我先开始演奏的！"

Pom is playing the piano louder.

'I was playing first!'

"但是我演奏得更好。"
乒乒的嗓门更大。

'But I play best.'
Pim shouts even louder.

这下，他们两个都在制造许多嘈杂的声音。
简直让人无法忍受！

They are both making so much noise.
It is unbearable!

可是，乒乒和乓乓却把自己当成了真正的著名音乐家，
就像在为无数观众演出似的！

**But Pim and Pom feel like they are real famous musicians,
performing for a big audience!**

"我是一位知名的钢琴家，我这一辈中最棒的。
我是乐队的灵魂，其他乐手都跟我弹！"

'I am a famous pianist. The greatest of my day.
I'm leader of the orchestra . They follow what I play!'

"不对，最赞的必定要数我！鼓手出来露个脸。
我是节奏的王者，地球上最棒的那一个！"

**'I'm the best, oh yes I am. The drummer in the band
I'm the king of rhythm. The greatest in the land!'**

"咳，乒乓，你的鼓点听起来太单调。
你看，我奏出的是美妙的旋律，钢琴弹出的才是音乐！"

'Your drumming is so dull, Pim. I hope you stop it soon.
It's me that plays the melody. The piano plays the tune.'

"接受现实，乒乓，承认失败吧。
要是没有我打鼓稳节奏，你方寸肯定会大乱！"

'You'll have to eat your words, Pom. And just admit defeat.
Without the rhythm of my drums, you'd start to lose the beat.'

"我们赶快来演奏吧。怎么回事，1，2，3？"
"我想，我的节奏乱了，你的旋律也走调了。"

'Let's play a tune now, quick. What was it, 1, 2, 3?'
'I think I've lost the rhythm, And you've lost the melody.'

幸好，一位指挥及时赶到。
他挥舞着指挥棒，而他们也能开始演奏了。

Luckily the conductor gets there just in time.
He counts off and they both start to play.

他们一同献上了一场真正的音乐会。

Together they put on a real show.

邻居狗狗凯斯负责弹贝司。

With Fred the neighbour's dog on the bass.

"嘿，乒乓，旋律真的很动听。"
"乒乓，这一下打得真出色。"

'Hey Pom, this tune is cool man.'
'Pim, what a groovy beat.'

"我们是绝配的爵士乐猫咪。"
"把最美的乐声来展现！"

'We're just a pair of jazz cats.'
'We'll make them tap their feet!'

哎呀，女主人来了。她很生气。
"乒乒，锅子怎么会放在这个地方？这些勺子又是怎么回事？

Oh dear, there's the Lady. She is angry.
'Pim, what's this pan doing here, and these spoons?'

"还有乒乓，你明明知道不许碰钢琴的！
快点儿走开，我要练习了。"

**'And Pom, you know you mustn't touch the piano.
Now off you get, I have to practice.'**

演奏音乐?

乒乒和乒乓更拿手哦，不是吗?

Making music?

Pim and Pom are much better, aren't they?